The Little

Written by Tanya Landman
Illustrated by Shoo Rayner

Collins

A little egg was in its nest.

Pick!

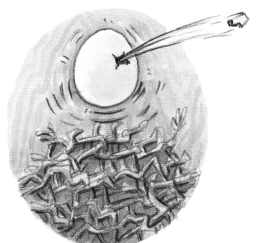

Peck!

Pock!

The little egg rolled down the straw and out of the barn.

Pick!

Peck!

Pock!

The little egg rolled down the hill and into the woods.

Pick!

Peck!

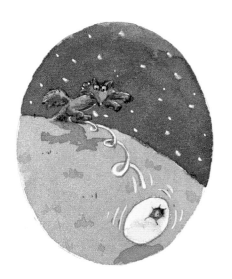

Pock!

The little egg rolled down a hole ...

... and shot out into the night.

The little egg hopped across a field ...

... and flew up into the sky.
Crack! CRACK! CRACK!

A little chick was in its nest.

Cheep! Cheep! Cheep!

Ideas for reading
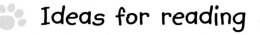

Written by Linda Pagett B.Ed (hons), M.Ed
Lecturer and Educational Consultant

Learning objectives: draw on grammatical awareness, to read with appropriate expression and intonation; use a range of strategies to work out, predict and check the meanings of unfamiliar words and to make sense of reading; notice differences between spoken and written forms through re-telling stories; describe story settings and incidents and relate to own experience; explore familiar themes and characters through improvisation and role-play

Curriculum links: Knowledge and Understanding of the World: life processes and living things; Science: Plants and animals in the local environment; life cycles

High frequency words: a, little, was, in, down, the, out, of, night, and, up

Interest words: pick, peck, pock, crack, cheep

Word count: 78

Resources: small whiteboard, pen

Getting started

- Look at the front and back covers together. Read the title and blurb and ask the children what the story might be about. *What hatches from an egg?*

- Walk through the book, discussing the illustrations. *What will happen to the little egg?*

- Read pp2-3 together, pointing to each word, and drawing attention to the words *Pick! Peck! Pock! What is happening to the egg on p3?*

Reading and responding

- Ask the children to read up to p13 together, with good expression. Pause at the end of each spread to predict what might happen next. *Where will the egg go? Will the fox eat the egg?*

- Encourage the children to use their phonic knowledge to decode unfamiliar words, e.g. look at initial letters, sound out the word and check understanding against the pictures.

- Discuss the events and outcome of the story. *What dangers did the egg face? How did it escape?*